for Sarah

First published in Great Britain by HarperCollins Publishers Ltd in 1996.
ISBN 0 00 761367 9 . Text and illustrations copyright © Rachel Pank 1996

Printed and bound in Singapore.

Little Big Sister

Rachel Pank

Collins

A Division of HarperCollins*Publishers*

This is little Lottie and her big sister Kate.
Kate says that because she's nearly four she wants to be grown-up.

Lottie wonders what Kate will do.
She follows her upstairs and into
Mummy and Daddy's bedroom.

"Those are Mummy's clothes,"
says Lottie.

Kate tries on a flowery dress.

Lottie helps Kate
do her hair.

She chooses some
shoes for Kate.

Kate puts on dingley dangley earrings, bangles, necklaces and a brooch.

And then the best bit of all,
Kate puts on her make-up.
Lottie just can't wait to help.

Pink lipstick and cream. Perfume and powder. Purple eye pencil.

"Let me," says Lottie.

"Shh!" whispers Kate,
"Mummy's coming!"

"Kate," cries Mummy,
"what are you doing?"

"Off with my clothes!"
"But Mum…" says Kate.
"Off with my shoes and
into the bath!"

"But I only wanted to be grown-up."

When Kate is clean and dry she goes to her room.

What is Lottie doing there?

She's trying on Kate's clothes!

"Off with my clothes!"
"But Kate..."
"Off with my shoes!"

"But I only wanted to be grown-up.
I want to be like YOU!" Lottie shouts.

"Do you really think I'm grown-up?"

"Of course you're grown-up,"
Lottie says, "because...

you're *my* BIG sister!"